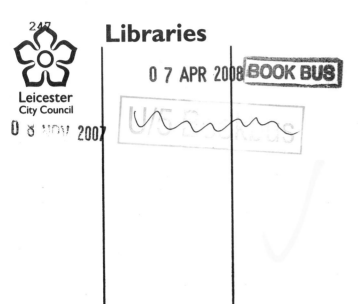

LBERG

other

steries

by

STUTZ

PUFFIN BOOKS

0140564039 4 398 FE

PUFFIN BOOKS
Published by the Penguin Group: London, New York, Australia, Canada and New Zealand
Penguin Books Ltd, Registered Offices: Harmondsworth, Middlesex, England

Published in Puffin Books 2001
1 3 5 7 9 10 8 6 4 2

Text copyright © Allan Ahlberg, 2001
Illustrations copyright © André Amstutz, 2001

The moral right of the author and illustrator has been asserted

Printed in Hong Kong by Imago Publishing Ltd

A CIP catalogue record for this book is available from the British Library

ISBN 0-140-56403-9

Mother Hen is on the phone.
"It is a mystery to me,"
she tells her friend.
"My chickens
won't eat their breakfast."

"My chickens won't eat their lunch.
My chickens won't eat their supper.
And yet they're getting . . .

fatter . . .

and fatter . . .

and FATTER!

I wonder why?"

The next day
Mother Hen
follows the chickens.

In the morning
the chickens find a little basket
in the yard.
"Ah!" says Mother Hen.

In the afternoon
the chickens find a little basket
in the orchard.
"Oh!" says Mother Hen.

In the evening
the chickens find
a little basket
by the river.
"Cluck!"
says Mother Hen.

"Some kind person
is making *free* picnics!
I wonder who?"

Slow Dog is also by the river.
He is fishing on the bridge.
Fast Fox is by the river too.
He is reading a book.

Yes.
Just reading a book.
That's all.

Just a nice . . .
little . . .
book!

The summer sun shines down.
The chickens doze off.

Mother Hen dozes off.
So does Slow Dog.

Fast Fox *rows* off.

See now! Fast Fox is fishing too.
Yes, that's all. Just fishing
with a nice . . .
little . . .   net!

Fast Fox catches chickens.
One chicken – yes!
Two chickens – yes, yes!
Three chickens – yes, yes, yes!

Row, row, row your boat,
Gently as can be,
Merrily, merrily, merrily, merrily
Chicken pie for me.

Mother Hen wakes up.
"Where are my chickens?"

Slow Dog wakes up.
"I've . . . got . . . a . . . bite."
Fast Fox *looks* up.

A fishing line
is dangling down.
Yes, that's all.
Just a nice . . .
little . . .
fishing line.

So the story ends.

Well, nearly.

Two days later
Mother Hen
phones her friend again.
"It is a mystery to me," she says.
"I seem to have an *extra* chicken.
Four chickens – yes.
I wonder . . ."

The End

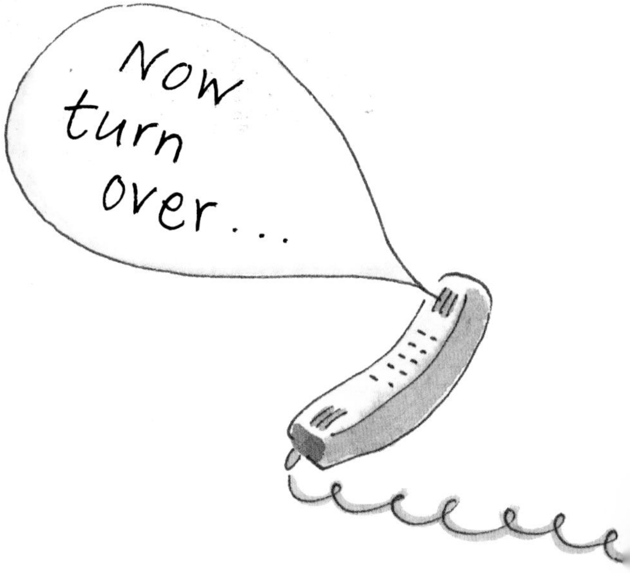
Now turn over...

THE FAST FOX, SLOW DOG BOOKS

Did you like this story?
Would you like to read another?
Try

Grandma Fox

In *Grandma Fox*,
Fast Fox dresses up . . .

as a grandma

a doctor

and a *postman*!

Oh no! Those poor little chickens . . .

. . . who can save them?